FOURTH OF JULY MICE!

FOURTH OF JULY MICE!

by Bethany Roberts

Illustrated by Doug Cushman

SCHOLASTIC INC.

New York   Toronto   London   Auckland   Sydney
Mexico City   New Delhi   Hong Kong   Buenos Aires

ISBN 0-439-78147-7

Text copyright © 2004 by Barbara Beverage.
Illustrations copyright © 2004 by Doug Cushman. All rights reserved.
Published by Scholastic Inc., 557 Broadway, New York, NY 10012,
by arrangement with Clarion Books. SCHOLASTIC and associated logos
are trademarks and/or registered trademarks of Scholastic Inc.

12 11 10 9 8 7 6 5 4   7 8 9 10/0

Printed in the U.S.A.   23

First Scholastic printing, May 2005

The illustrations were executed in watercolor.

The text was set in 24-point Stone Informal.

Happy Birthday, America!
—B.R.

To Leonard Everett Fisher—painter, patriot, teacher, and friend
—D.C.

Parading mice
march left, right, left.

Waving flags,
red, white, and blue!

Bang! Toot! Clang!
Happy Fourth!

Mr. Mouse
marches too.

Hungry mice
left, right . . . stop!

It's time to eat.
What's for lunch?

Sunflower seeds!
Pass the cheese!

Munch, munch,
crunch, crunch, crunch!

Now let's play!
Toss the ball.

Whack, smack,
run, run, run!

15

Let's have a race!
Four mice in sacks

hop, hop, plop.
Oh, what fun!

17

Three hot mice
in red, white, blue

plunk, dunk,
one, two, three.

One scared mouse
stays on the bank,
shaking, quaking.

"No, not me!"

Three wet mice
dip, float, glide.

Drip, flop, flip,
splash, splosh, slide.

23

One dry mouse suns on a rock.
Mr. Mouse sails—glide, ride.

"Stop, Mr. Mouse! You've gone too far!"
Oh, no! What to do?

A brave little mouse
jumps right in.

"I can swim!"
"Three cheers for you!"

Four happy mice
sparkle on a log.

Is mouse fun done
this July Fourth day?

Look in the sky . . .
BOOM! BOOM! BOOM!

We love America!
Hooray! Hooray!